JPK

CIP Data is available.

Published in the United States 1997
by Dutton Children's Books,
a division of Penguin Books USA Inc.
375 Hudson Street, New York, New York 10014
Originally published in Great Britain 1996 by
Hamish Hamilton Ltd, London
Typography by Julia Goodman
Printed in Italy
First American Edition
ISBN 0-525-45722-4
1 3 5 7 9 10 8 6 4 2

DAISY IS A MOMMY

LISA KOPPER

Dutton Children's Books ✦ NEW YORK

Morris, Dolores, and
Little Daisy have a mommy.

Their mommy is Daisy.

Baby has a mommy, too.

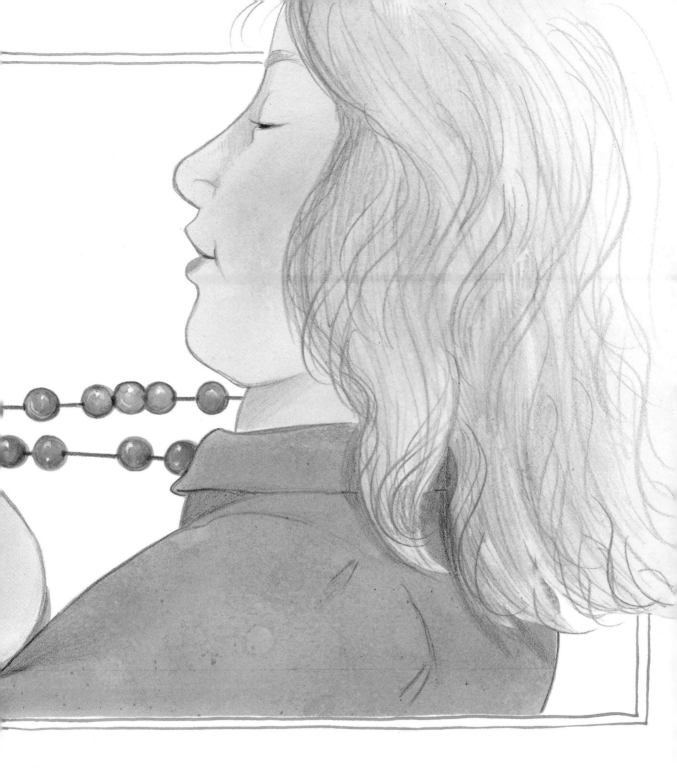

In the morning, Mommy
gets her baby out of bed.

So does Daisy.

Mommy carries her baby
to the kitchen.

So does Daisy.

Mommy gives her baby
the best breakfast.

So does Daisy.

Mommy gives her baby
a bath.

So does Daisy.

Mommy and Daisy watch
all the babies play.

Mommy cleans up her
baby's mess.

But Daisy doesn't.

Daisy goes upstairs.

And so do all the babies.

Mommy looks for Daisy
and the babies.

Are they in Baby's bed? NO!

Are they in Daisy's bed? NO!

They are in Mommy's bed!

Daisy is sound asleep.

And now, so is everybody else.

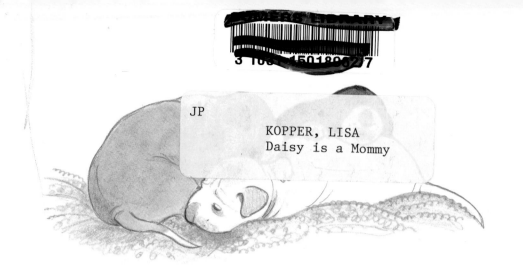